About This Book

Thank you so much for your support for *Give Please a Chance,* a book that I felt was important for children in many ways. Hearing all your messages about how it has inspired a higher degree of courtesy and manners was very encouraging,
so I decided to keep going!
Saying "thank you" can be something that children do automatically without thinking much about what it means. This book shows how we can feel gratitude for so many things—not just for birthday presents, but even for the simplest things in our lives.
Kids know when to say thank you—this book will tell them why.
Thank you for sharing this book with your kids and grandkids.

—James Patterson

JAMES PATTERSON

GIVE THANK YOU A TRY

JIMMY PATTERSON BOOKS
LITTLE, BROWN AND COMPANY
NEW YORK BOSTON LONDON

Every morning our family has breakfast together. It's nice. Daddy
and Mommy always say: "**Thank you** for being Emma."
"**Thank you** for being Olivia."

"**Thank you** for being Jimmy." And we say:
"**Thank you** for being Mommy and Daddy."

Illustrated by Elizabet Vukovic

Thank you for . . . PB&Js in our PJs.

Illustrated by Jeff Ebbeler

Thank you for . . . miles and miles and miles of smiles and smiles and smiles.

Illustrated by Louise Forshaw

Thank you for . . . raindrops that keep falling on our heads, and toes, and everywhere in between.

Illustrated by Tracy Dockray

Thank you for . . . the petting zoo. Woo-hoo!

Illustrated by Jeff Ebbeler

We say "**please**" and "**thank you**" in our house. When Isabella was teeny-weeny, we taught her "**please** and **thank you.**" She would sit in her high chair and say,

"**Please** and **thank you, please** and **thank you,**" over and over. I think she was saying she was hungry.

Illustrated by Cori Doerrfeld

Thank you for . . . blue skies, nothing but blue skies. Oh, and clouds shaped like horses, cows, and monkeys!

Illustrated by Jennifer Zivoin

Thank you for . . . SNOW . . . and sleigh rides . . . and snowballs . . . and snow girls.

Illustrated by Jordan Wray

Thank you for . . . tickles, tickles, tickles!

Illustrated by Ryan Wheatcroft

Thank you for . . . my teddy bear, who also says "**thank you**."

Illustrated by Kate Babok

We have a very special teacher at school. When the bell rings after class, he stands at the door.

He says **"thank you"** to each of us when we leave.

Illustrated by John Nez

Thank you for . . . the night-light in the hall, and the one on the stairs, and the one in the bathroom.

Illustrated by Donald Wu

Thank you for . . . tricky, terrible, totally tough tongue twisters.

Illustrated by John Nez

Mommy was in the hospital (she's okay now). Our family visited her there after her operation. Mommy woke up. She saw us. Then she smiled and said, "Thank you, thank you, thank you—for being here." Everybody cried.

Illustrated by Chelen Ecija

Thank you for . . . hills and dales and humongous whales.

Illustrated by Bao Luu

Thank you for . . . Santa telling Mommy her Christmas present came from both of us.

Illustrated by Luke Flowers

Thank you for . . . sweet puppy licks and cozy kitten cuddles. Nothing could be better!

Illustrated by Ruth Galloway

Thank you for . . . holding me way, way up high to see the Thanksgiving parade.

Illustrated by Julia Kuo

One time we went to my brother's baseball game. He struck out. My brother doesn't ever strike out. His team lost. My brother was real quiet going home after the game. Usually he's noisy. I whispered to him,

"You're a really good baseball player, Matt." My brother stayed quiet. Then he said, "**Thank you**, Sophie." We were both quiet after that.

Illustrated by Jomike Tejido

Thank you for . . . spinach, kale, and broccoli.

But **thank you** especially for ice-cream sundaes with whipped cream and a cherry on top!

Illustrated by Julie Robine

A famous football player grew up in our town. He came to visit one day. Just about the whole town went to see him at the high school stadium. He said he came back home just to say **"thank you."**

Illustrated by Alejandro O'Kif

Thank you for . . . my toasty-warm, comfy beddy-bye, and my "lovey" to snuggle with me.

Illustrated by Cori Doerrfeld

Every night before we go to bed, Daddy and Mommy say:
"**Thank you** for being Emma." "**Thank you** for being Olivia."
"**Thank you** for being Jimmy."

And we say: "**Thank you** for being Mommy and Daddy. **Thank you** and good night."

Illustrated by Elizabet Vukovic

Text copyright © 2017 by James Patterson

Illustrations copyright © 2017 by: Kate Babok, pages 20–21; Tracy Dockray, pages 8–9; Cori Doerrfeld, pages 12–13, 44–45; Jeff Ebbeler, pages 4–5, 10–11; Chelen Ecija, pages 28–29; Luke Flowers, pages 32–33; Louise Forshaw, pages 6–7; Ruth Galloway, pages 34–35; Julia Kuo, pages 36–37; Bao Luu, pages 30–31; John Nez, pages 22–23, 26–27; Alejandro O'Kif, pages 42–43; Julie Robine, pages 40–41; Jomike Tejido, pages 38–39; Elizabet Vukovic, pages 2–3, 46–47; Ryan Wheatcroft, pages 18–19; Jordan Wray, pages 16–17; Donald Wu, pages 24–25; Jennifer Zivoin, pages 14–15

JIMMY Patterson Books / Little, Brown and Company
Hachette Book Group
1290 Avenue of the Americas, New York, NY 10104
jimmypatterson.org

First Edition: October 2017

JIMMY Patterson Books is an imprint of Little, Brown and Company, a division of Hachette Book Group, Inc. The Little, Brown name and logo are trademarks of Hachette Book Group, Inc. The JIMMY Patterson® name and logo are trademarks of JBP Business, LLC.

The publisher is not responsible for websites (or their content) that are not owned by the publisher.

The Hachette Speakers Bureau provides a wide range of authors for speaking events. To find out more, go to hachettespeakersbureau.com or call (866) 376-6591.

Library of Congress Cataloging-in-Publication Data

Name: Patterson, James, author.
Title: Give thank you a try / James Patterson.
Description: First edition. | New York : Little, Brown and Company, 2017. |
"JIMMY Patterson Books." | Summary: An illustrated exploration of the
phrase "thank you" and the many scenarios of kindness and gratitude in
which it can be used.
Identifiers: LCCN 2017002945 | ISBN 9780316440424 (hc) | ISBN 9780316440455 (library edition ebook)
Subjects: | CYAC: Gratitude—Fiction.
Classification: LCC PZ7.1.O68 Gl 2017 | DDC [E]—dc23 LC record available at https://lccn.loc.gov/2017002945

10 9 8 7 6 5 4 3 2 1

Imago

Printed in China